THIS BOOK BELONGS TO

kelsbton
stoo
mol ye

First published in hardback in Great Britain by
HarperCollins Children's Books in 2010

1 3 5 7 9 10 8 6 4 2

ISBN: 978-0-00-736274-5

HarperCollins Children's Books is a division of HarperCollins Publishers Ltd.

Text by Alison Sage
Text copyright © HarperCollins Publishers Ltd 2010
Illustrations copyright © Sarah Gibb 2010

Visit our website at www.harpercollins.co.uk

Printed in China

RAPUNZEL

Sarah Gibb

Based on the original story by
The Brothers Grimm

HarperCollins *Children's Books*

Many years ago, in a beautiful country, far away, there lived a young gardener and his pretty wife. They were very happy, except for one thing. They longed for a child.

At last, one day, the wife found she was going to have a baby.

"How could we want anything else in the world?" cried her husband joyfully.

But the young wife fell ill and she grew paler and sicker until it seemed she was going to die. "There is only one thing that would save me," she whispered, "and that is a fresh salad picked from the garden next door that I can see from our window."

Then the young man grew very afraid. Next to their little cottage was a walled garden, with beautiful trees and plants of all kinds. Spring blossom cascaded from the trees and little green leaves peeped out through the cracks between the walls. But this was an enchanted garden belonging to a witch who was so cruel that no one had ever entered it and lived.

Every day, the young wife looked out of her window longingly at the sweet green leaves. And every day she grew weaker.

One night, the young man could bear it no longer and he crept out of their cottage and slipped over the wall into the magic garden, cool and

blue in the moonlight. Shaking, he snatched a couple of handfuls of salad leaves and scrambled back to safety.

In the morning, colour came back to his wife's pale cheeks as she ate the delicious crisp leaves and she fell back on her pillow, sighing, "If only I could eat that salad just once more, I would be completely well."

The gardener climbed the witch's wall again that night. He was bending down to pick the leaves when suddenly a harsh voice said, "So, *you* are the thief that steals my salad!"

Terrified, he fell at the witch's feet. "Let me go," he cried, "I did it to save my wife!" And he babbled that the salad was a miraculous cure.

The witch smiled at him cruelly. "I'll let you live, and you can take as much salad as your wife needs – but only if you make me this promise: when the baby is born, it's MINE!"

The young man was too frightened to speak so he simply nodded and scuttled away.

When he got home his wife was delighted with the salad and as soon as she'd eaten it she was completely well again. But the gardener did not tell her of his promise. He was too ashamed.

Spring faded into summer and at the end of that a baby girl was born. The young husband had not forgotten about the witch, and he watched anxiously as his friends and relations came to give them presents and congratulations.

All of a sudden, the door flew open and in stormed the witch. "I've come for my child!" she laughed, and snatching up the baby, she whirled out of the cottage before the horrified guests could move or speak. The poor parents wept, but there was nothing they could do. The witch had vanished with their daughter.

The witch called the baby Rapunzel and took her to a secret castle. Rapunzel was a pretty child, always laughing and playing and as the years passed she grew more and more beautiful. Her

long hair was a shining waterfall of gold, and her eyes sparkled like twin stars. The witch watched her closely, noticing how even the birds of the air and the little creatures of the forest fell in love with her.

One day, the witch took Rapunzel by the hand and led her into the forest, muttering, "You're too beautiful for your own good!"

"Where are we going?" asked Rapunzel innocently as the witch led her down secret paths, deeper and deeper into the trees.

Suddenly they came to a clearing and there in the middle was a tall tower, with no door; just a few windows at the very top.

"This is your new home!" cried the witch gleefully. "No one will ever find you here, except me!"

To Rapunzel's amazement, although the tower was as slender as a tree, inside there was room after beautiful room, lit by thousands of delicate lamps which glowed as bright as day. Right at the top of the tower was a tiny balcony and Rapunzel's friends, the birds, who had followed her through the forest, gathered to greet her and eat out of her hand.

The forest creatures were sorry for the beautiful girl locked away from the world and spent many hours playing with her as she wandered from room to room in the enchanted tower.

Every morning the witch came to visit, and as there were no doors, she had worked out a special system. She would arrive at the tower and call out, "Rapunzel, Rapunzel, let down your golden hair!"

And Rapunzel would come to the edge of the tower, unfasten her glorious braid and send it tumbling down to the witch below. The old woman would nimbly scramble up the smooth side of the tower, clinging on to Rapunzel's hair as if it were a rope. Then the two would have breakfast together.

In this way several years passed until, eventually, Rapunzel began to grow bored with her prison. She had everything she could want – and yet the days seemed to pass so slowly as she sat at the top of the tower, singing sadly to herself and combing her long hair.

One morning, the son of the neighbouring prince was out riding. It was such a beautiful day that he wandered this way and that until he found himself in a part of the forest he had never seen before.

All of a sudden, he heard the sound of singing and he followed it, curious to discover who owned such a lovely voice. To his amazement he saw a tower, and at the very top was the most beautiful girl he had ever seen.

He was just about to call out to her, when the bushes parted and an old woman appeared. Something in her expression made the prince shrink back into the trees and he watched as she cried out, "Rapunzel, Rapunzel, let down your golden hair!"

Straight away the beautiful girl unfastened her hair and it flooded down to the old woman below, who climbed up the tower and in through the window.

"Aha! So that's how it is!" thought the young man.

He waited patiently out of sight until, at last, the witch had gone away. Then he went to the foot of the tower and called out, just as she had, "Rapunzel, Rapunzel, let down your golden hair!"

And exactly as before, the beautiful girl lowered down her braid and, holding on tightly, the young prince leapt lightly up the tower.

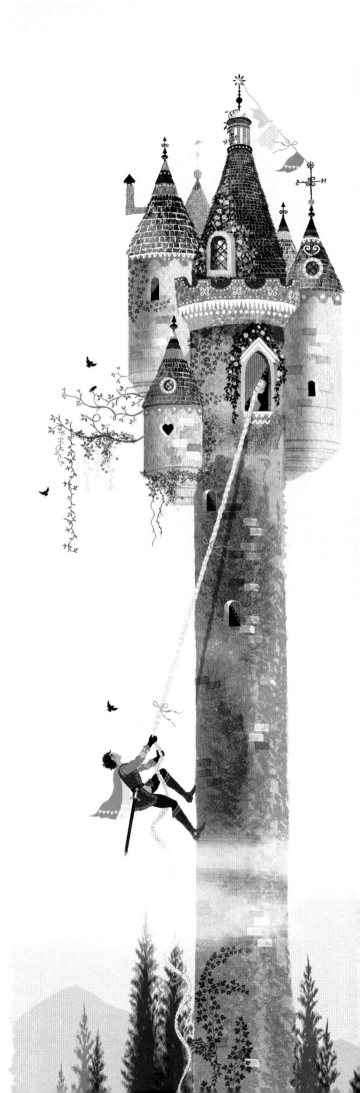

Rapunzel was both amazed and scared when the prince appeared. But he smiled at her in such a friendly way and he spoke so pleasantly that soon they were talking and laughing together as if they had always known each other. The hours flew past and all too soon it was time for the prince to slip away, back to his palace.

Rapunzel knew instinctively that it would be dangerous to mention the young prince and so she said nothing when the witch returned the next day. But her heart was in her mouth when, as soon as she was alone again, he was at the foot of the tower, calling to her to lower her hair once more.

After that, time seemed to pass much more swiftly for Rapunzel as she and the prince spent longer together, talking and playing with her forest friends.

Soon she and the prince fell deeply in love and they began to talk about escaping. Rapunzel had thought up a clever plan…

She asked the witch for some gold thread to weave a special dress. Then, each day, as soon as the witch had left, she also wove a long rope that she could use to climb down the tower one day.

Whenever they met, Rapunzel and the prince talked of what they would do once they'd left the tower and it amazed Rapunzel to learn of all the strange and wonderful things that were waiting for her in the world outside.

Every morning, Rapunzel could hardly wait for the old witch to leave so that her prince could arrive. Until, one day, the witch began to watch her suspiciously, puzzled at her new-found sparkle. But Rapunzel was in another world and she didn't notice.

"It's strange," she mused dreamily, "you take so long to climb up the tower these days. The prince almost seems to *fly* up to me!"

The witch stared in stunned horror. She could hardly believe her ears. "*Snake!* You've betrayed me!" she screeched. "There's no punishment good enough for you!" In a terrible rage, she grabbed hold of a huge pair of scissors and hacked off Rapunzel's beautiful braid, tying it to the balcony of the tower. Then she drove Rapunzel out into the forest, hoping that wild animals would attack her, or that she would starve.

But the forest creatures were sorry for their lovely friend and they protected her instead. They fed her on nuts and berries and showed her spring water to drink. Poor Rapunzel was in a daze of misery and she cried and cried. She was frightened for her prince, wondering whether the witch had hurt him and whether they would ever see each other again.

Meanwhile, the prince, not suspecting any danger, went to the tower and called out, "Rapunzel, Rapunzel, let down your golden hair!"

The hair fell down around him as usual and he climbed up. But there, staring at him with the most hideous expression, was the old witch, grasping the other end of his dear Rapunzel's hair.

"What have you done to Rapunzel?" he cried.

"You've lost her for ever!" shrieked the old woman. And she pushed the young prince so hard, he fell from the tower. He tumbled down into a thorn bush and was so badly hurt that he could no longer see.

Overcome with pain and misery, he pulled himself up and staggered into the forest with the evil witch's curse ringing in his ears.

The prince hadn't gone far, when he suddenly realised he was not alone. There was a deer at his knees, guiding him so that he didn't tumble into ditches or bump into trees. Then a little bird landed on his shoulder and young foxes trotted along at his other side, gently shepherding him so that he kept to the path.

"Who are you?" he asked, and it seemed that somehow the spirit of his dear Rapunzel was with him, helping him in his pain. In the evening, the creatures led him to a bed of soft moss and in the morning, they nuzzled him gently awake.

The prince wandered for days in this way, more dead than alive, still hoping against hope that he might find Rapunzel.

Then one morning, while he was wandering in a fog of pain, he heard a beautiful voice singing a sad song about her long-lost love. It was his Rapunzel! The forest animals had led him to her. He shouted with joy and stumbled towards the sound of her voice.

Rapunzel was horrified to see how badly hurt he was and she wept to see his poor eyes. The prince lifted his hands to touch her face. As he did so, her tears fell on his eyelids and, magically, they were healed. He could see again!

The two of them were so happy they could hardly find the breath to tell each other. Rapunzel was alternately crying and laughing to think of everything the prince had suffered and of the wonderful future that stretched ahead of them.

With the help of their forest friends, they found their way back to the prince's kingdom, where a huge feast was planned to celebrate his return. The prince and Rapunzel soon decided to turn it into a wedding feast and invited everyone from many miles around.

Rapunzel's parents heard of the celebration and when they saw the new princess and heard her strange story they realised it must be their long-lost daughter. And they wept tears of pure joy that she was alive and well.

As for the witch, she was so bitter and angry, she shut herself away in a gloomy castle and never showed her face in that country again.

Time passed happily for Rapunzel and the prince, and every now and then they would slip away from the kingdom and into the enchanted forest to spend a sunny afternoon with the forest creatures – friends they would never forget.